First published 2005 by Walker Books Ltd, 87 Vauxhall Walk, London SE11 5HJ

2 4 6 8 10 9 7 5 3 1

© 2005 Kanako Usui

The right of Kanako Usui to be identified as author/illustrator of this work has been asserted
by her in accordance with the Copyright, Designs and Patents Act 1988

This book has been typeset in Futura-Book

Printed in China

British Library Cataloguing in Publication Data: a catalogue record for this book is available from the British Library

ISBN 1-84428-023-3

www.walkerbooks.co.uk

LAZY SANTA & TOTO

How a sheep and a stray sneeze saved Christmas

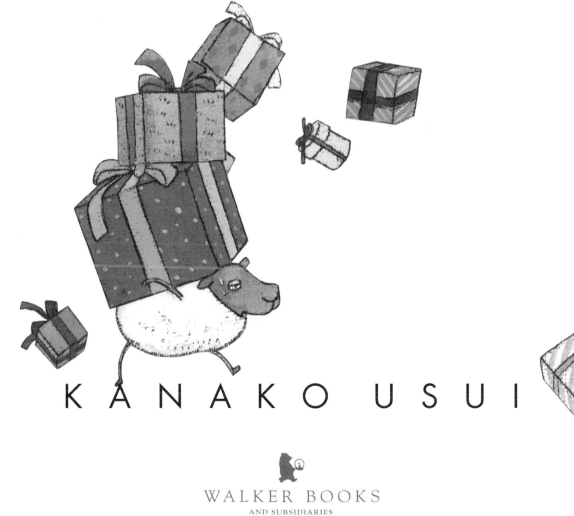

K A N A K O   U S U I

WALKER BOOKS
AND SUBSIDIARIES
LONDON • BOSTON • SYDNEY • AUCKLAND

IN THE FARTHEST LAND OF ALL THE WORLD,
where no one ever goes, Santa lived with a little
sheep called Toto.

Santa was very lazy, and Toto had to do all the work. Month after month he read the letters sent from children all over the world, to see what they wanted for Christmas.

When the chill wind began to
blow, Toto ordered the presents
from the Ducky Toy Company.

When winter came, Toto wrapped
them up in paper and put them
away until Christmas Eve.

On top of all this, Toto had to look after the reindeer and do all the housework. Meanwhile, Santa was busy being lazy.

But Toto didn't complain.

Christmas Eve came at last. This was the only day when Santa had to do any work, but he still got up late.

He went to the bathroom to brush his beard.

But he was so sleepy, he picked up a razor by mistake!

"Oh, nooooo! I've shaved off my beard!"

Santa couldn't deliver the presents without a beard!

Suddenly he had an idea. He grabbed Toto and stuck him on his nose. Then he put on his red Christmas suit, and the sack of presents. With his new sheep-beard in place, Santa set off.

Toto didn't complain.

Santa and Toto sped through the night with sleigh bells ringing.

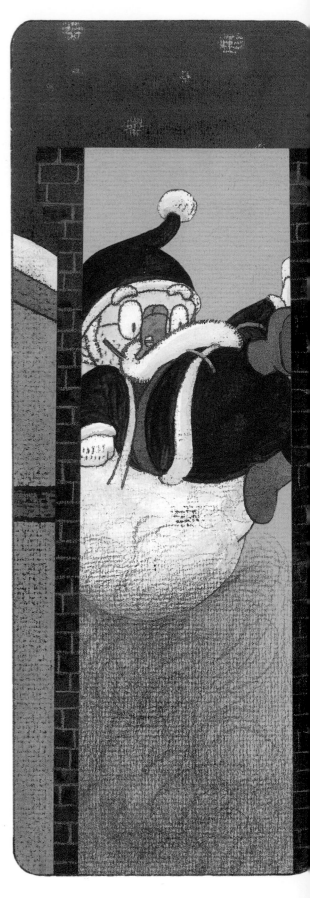

At the
first
house,
Santa
climbed
down the
chimney.
It was
very, very
sooty,
and it
tickled
his nose!

Ha…

Haa…

Hatchoooo!

With an almighty sneeze, Toto was blown off Santa's face and shot out of the fireplace. He landed in the middle of a little girl's bedroom.

"Wow! A sheep!" said the little girl. "Just what I wanted!"

She gave Santa a hug to say
thank you, and promised to
take good care of Toto.

Santa didn't know what to
say, but the little girl was
so happy, he decided to
leave Toto with her.

And Toto didn't complain.

Santa worked alone for the rest of the night, but without his beard he kept being mistaken for a robber.

Back home everything started to go wrong. Santa couldn't cook.

The reindeer didn't like him.

And he had no idea what to do with the letters.

It wasn't long before
Santa realized how much
he had depended on
Toto for everything.

The very next day
Santa received
a letter from Toto.

Dear Santa

Hello! How are you? It's been

a while since Christmas.

I enjoy playing with the girl.

Her name is Coco. She feeds me well.

I'm happy here. Hope

you are well too.

Toto x x

DEAR TOTO

THANK YOU FOR YOUR LETTER.
I AM GLAD THAT YOU ARE HAPPY
WITH COCO. I AM FINE. MY
BEARD HAS ALMOST GROWN BACK.
I WANT TO SAY "THANK YOU"
FOR EVERYTHING YOU DID FOR ME,
AND I PROMISE I WILL TRY NOT TO BE
LAZY ANY MORE.
KEEP IN TOUCH.
LOVE SANTA

Toto was very happy
to hear that Santa had
turned over a new leaf.

However...

Helper Wanted

Year round help needed with domestic chores - Includes some paperwork. Applicants must be fond of reindeer.
Please contact
S. Clause
77 Jingle St.

PROMISE YOU'LL KEEP THIS A SECRET,
but I heard that Santa employed a penguin recently...

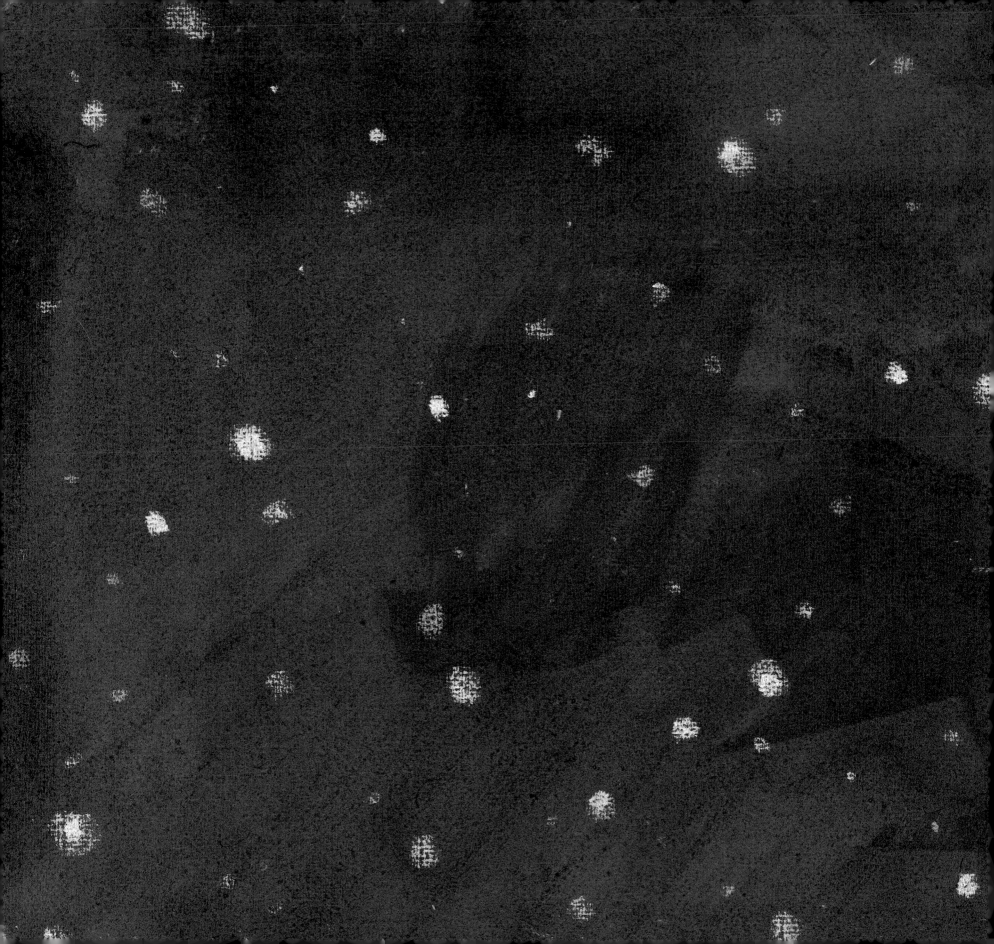